LEW WALLACE

BOY WRITER

Written by
Martha E. Schaaf

Illustrate
Cathy Mc

ISBN 978-1-882859-054 hardback
ISBN 978-1-882859-061 paperback

Patria Press, Inc.
PO Box 752
Carmel, IN 46082
Website: www.patriapress.com

Printed and bound in the United States of America

Text originally published by the Bobbs-Merrill Co., 1961, in the
Childhood of Famous Americans Series® The Childhood of Famous
American Series® is a registered trademark of Simon & Schuster, Inc.

Library of Congress Cataloging-in-Publication Data

Schaaf, Martha E.
Lew Wallace, boy writer / written by
Martha E. Schaaf; illustrated by Cathy Morrison.
   p. cm. — (young patriots series ; 3)
SUMMARY: Fictionalized biography of the boyhood and youth of
a great nephew of John Paul Jones who, after his boyhood on the
frontier, grew up to be an inventor, novelist, and statesman.
   ISBN: 9781882859054 (hardcover) — 9781882859061 (pbk.)
   1. Wallace, Lew, 1827–1905—Childhood and youth— Juvenile
fiction. [1. Wallace, Lew, 1827–1905— Childhood and youth—Fiction.
   2. Authors, American—Fiction. 3. Statesman—Fiction.] I. Morrison,
Cathy, ill. II. Title. III. Series.

Edited by Harold Underdown
Design by Timothy Mayer/TM Design

Contents

Illustrations

Publisher's Note

The term "Native American" has replaced the term "Indian" in modern times, and we recognize and applaud its use. However, during the time depicted in this book, the term in popular usage was "Indian," and the reader will notice the word used several times in the text. It is not our intention to offend anyone by the use of "Indian." We have kept the term as written in the original version of the story as we feel it is important to stay historically accurate and true to the time period portrayed.

*"To all those who made it possible,
this book is affectionately dedicated."*

Chapter 1

Little Hero

"Wake up, my little dreamer!" A tall woman knelt beside her young son, asleep in a trundle bed.

"Wake up," she whispered again. It was early, earlier than her son usually woke up. The boy stirred slightly. He felt her hand gently brushing back his hair. "Come, Lewis, get up! We are moving today!"

His dark eyes opened wide, and he sat up suddenly. Now he remembered his father had said they would be going with the big, white-topped wagons this trip!

Lewis Wallace liked to watch the wagon trains as they came rumbling through their town, Brookville, Indiana, on the road leading west. Sometimes they stopped at his grandfather's inn.

"Are we going in a wagon?" Lewis asked.

"No, we will go in the carriage, Lewis," Mrs. Wallace replied. "It is already harnessed and packed. Get into your clothes."

Lewis heard his younger brothers, three-year-old

John and Baby Edwin, in the next room.

"William is already up," his mother called, as she hurried to the younger children.

"Of course he is," Lewis thought. Older brother William always did everything right. Lewis loved his brother Bill and tried to be like him, but Lewis was different.

Now he was thinking of the wagons. He listened for their sound—bells on the harness tinkling in rhythm with the clomp, clomp of the hoof beats. He could hear them coming.

"Ready, Lewis?" his mother called.

"Almost," he answered, quickly pulling on the homespun trousers. They felt scratchy but he was pleased he no longer had to wear a dress. Lewis had grown into trousers on his fifth birthday, a few weeks past. When asked his age, he would proudly reply, "I am five. I was born on April 10, 1827, and I am grownup! See my trousers?"

Now dressed, Lewis went over to the open window to look for the wagons. Upstairs here, in their tall brick house, he was a giant looking over the world below him.

The sun was coming up over the hills to the southeast, touching everything with gold. The river was splashing over the wheel of one of the mills. The gold eagle on top of the Court House steeple caught his eye. The Court House bell reflected the golden rays.

His father spent much of his time there. Mr. Wallace helped people who needed a lawyer.

Lewis wondered if there would be a court house where they were moving. He looked at the hills to the west. They looked golden, too. Then he glanced down.

Yes, the carriage was waiting below, with trunks and bundles piled on top. The horses were tied to the hitching post. They pulled and strained at it, impatient to be off.

He looked at the heavy rear wheels of the carriage. A stone was propped under one of them as an extra brake. Slowly the stone began to move, tugged by a small hand.

Lewis' heart stood still.

"John must be under the carriage," he thought, "playing by the big wheel!"

"John, John," Lewis screamed, as he saw his little brother so close to danger. Dashing out of the room, Lewis slid down the banister, ran out the door, and stooped under the back of the carriage.

With all his strength, Lewis pulled John away, just as the stone loosened. The carriage jolted forward. John yelled. The horses reared and jerked free of the post. The horses were running away with the loaded carriage! Lewis ran after the carriage.

With all his strength, Lewis pulled John away . . .

"Stop the horses! Stop the horses!" he yelled.

Heads popped out of the stately houses along the street. Almost breathless, Lewis kept running and shouting. The horses were at the corner of the Town Square now. With two roads to choose from, the horses slowed.

In the second that they seemed to pause, a tall man leaped in front of them. He tugged at the reins to stop them.

"Whoa, Ball, whoa. Easy now," he commanded firmly.

The horses reared. The carriage reeled, shook, and came to a sudden stop.

Lewis ran to catch up with them. The horses were in front of Grandfather Wallace's inn, at the southeast corner of the Square. The man who had stopped the runaways was his grandfather!

"Grandfather!" Lewis shouted, "You stopped the horses!"

"I heard you from the doorway. When I came out I saw you pull John from under the carriage," Grandfather Wallace explained.

Grandmother Wallace appeared at the door. "What is all the commotion, Andrew?"

"I heard Lewis shouting to his brother. The next thing I knew, the carriage was racing down the street headed this way. I just ran out and stopped it."

"Wasn't Grandfather brave?" exclaimed Lewis.

"Lewis, you were the brave one," Grandfather Wallace replied. "I saw you rescue John."

"Well, bravery just runs in the family!" Grandmother Wallace exclaimed. "Our Lewis might be as famous as brave Uncle John, someday," she said, smiling down at her grandson.

Hearing those words, Lewis found his breath, and his chest swelled with pride. He dreamed of being a hero like his great-great-uncle John Paul Jones—a real hero!

Lewis's grandmother interrupted his thoughts. "Is my little hero hungry? Come in and have a bite of breakfast, Lewis. There'll be none at your house this morning. Your mother must have all the kettles packed by now." Grandmother bustled off into the Inn.

Lewis grinned. He always liked to eat at his grandfather's inn, and to watch the square dancing. He glanced at the sign over the door: THE BROOKVILLE HOTEL. ANDREW WALLACE, PROPRIETOR.

"And what may I serve you, my good man?" Grandfather was treating him like a traveler, bowing and ushering him inside.

"Bed and board, sir, and lodging for my horses." Lewis remembered the words of the travelers. "And how much is the fare?" he added. He enjoyed pretending to be a real guest.

"Seventy-five cents for both of you, and the food is the best known in this part of the country. Come, sit down and I will call the boy to bring your breakfast."

Lewis sat on a bench at the long plank table, in the rear of the big room. A group of travelers was having breakfast here.

"They are talking about land again," Lewis thought. He preferred hearing tales of adventure, like those about Daniel Boone, or George Rogers Clark, or perhaps his father's favorite, William Henry Harrison. Lewis knew that those men met at an inn like his grandfather's, and planned campaigns while they ate.

Suddenly the young traveler felt hungry. He looked up at the fat hams and bunches of herbs, which hung from the rafters. Smells of buckwheat cakes came from the kitchen hearth.

"Good morning, Lewis," the hotel boy said, as he set a plateful of the steaming cakes in front of Lewis.

Grandfather Wallace came to sit down beside Lewis.

"Grandfather, will there be any Indians where we are going?" Lewis asked while he ate his breakfast. His grandfather always knew everything. In Cincinnati he had published books and a newspaper.

"Black Hawk is around somewhere—trying to

stir up the friendly Indians. The West isn't won yet. You may help tame it someday!" replied Grandfather Wallace.

The boy's eyes sparkled. "Will we live in a wigwam?" he asked.

"Not a wigwam—more likely a cabin. There will be no fine houses like these in Brookville. But you might be living in the governor's mansion in a few years," Grandfather suggested.

"Gov-er-nor's man-shun? What's a governor's mansion?" Lewis was quite interested.

"Oh, a fine house, something like the Noble house here, or even your own, where your grandfather Test lived before he left. Those were the days! Brookville was the biggest town in Indiana when I came here," Grandfather replied.

"That was only fifteen years ago, in 1817, the year after Indiana became a state. Brookville was booming. The court house was just being built, and houses, too; brick houses right here next to the wilderness. Mills were humming night and day along the Whitewater River."

"Why are people leaving now, Grandfather?"

"The Government Land Office was moved—everybody's after more land, and money," Andrew Wallace explained with a sigh. "Some of the mills have closed because there are no roads or canals to carry the products to market, and the river's too shallow since the trees have been cut."

"Is there a river and a court house where we are going?" inquired Lewis.

"Oh, yes, your father couldn't practice law without a court house. Covington is the busiest town on the Wabash, the biggest river in Indiana, but you might be living in Indianapolis soon."

"Ind-i-an-a-po-lis?" Lewis pronounced the big word slowly.

"Yes, Indianapolis is the capital of Indiana. Your father is lieutenant governor of Indiana now. That's only one step from being governor. You might be living in the governor's mansion, and then—"

"Who is talking about a governor's mansion?" A strong, clear voice interrupted. It was the lieutenant governor himself.

David Wallace usually dressed properly in black broadcloth, with a stiff white shirt front. Today Lewis saw that his father wore a hunter's buck-skin jacket. He would be driving the heavily loaded carriage.

"Well, son, where have you been? You missed the excitement a while back," Andrew Wallace said.

"I was at the Court House to pick up my books, but I heard the noise and looked out. By the time I reached the window, the carriage was too far down the street for me to stop it. I knew my good horse Ball would go back to her stable here. You did well to stop the carriage, father."

"What do you mean, I did well? Your son did well. John might have been killed, if not for him. Little John was playing under the carriage, pulling the stone braking the rear wheel. Lewis saw John's danger and pulled John away from under the wheels," Grandfather Wallace explained.

"Why, Lewis, that was quick thinking."

Grandmother looked in from the kitchen. "Is that all you can say about your son?" she exclaimed. "Lewis is a little hero!"

The Little Hero looked down at his feet for a moment, then jumped up.

"Come on, Father, let's get started!" he said.

Chapter 2

The Journey

The sun was high over the Court House when the Wallace family finally started.

"May I ride on top with you, Father?" Lewis asked. His father boosted Lewis to the driver's seat of the carriage and climbed up himself. Bill traveled inside the carriage, helping his mother with John and the baby.

"Don't forget us," one of the neighbors called out.

"We'll put this town on the map again," the Lieutenant Governor replied, as he tapped the horses. The carriage went at a brisk pace, and the town was soon hidden by the hills.

Lewis looked ahead. There were many travelers on the road today. Stagecoaches and wagons wheels rolled over the dusty, corded road. Through creek beds and stump-littered trails they went. Fields of ripening wheat, green meadows, and deep forests still untouched by ax and plow lay before them.

"Father, how long will our journey be?"

"The stagecoach makes the trip to Indianapolis in two days now. That is hard driving, and just half way to Covington. We have more than a week of rough travel to get there. In a few years, though, we will build canals and roads that will make traveling easier. The map already shows them. Here, son, look at it," answered Mr. Wallace.

David Wallace took a folded paper from his pocket. "The Traveler's Guide Through Indiana," he announced. "See if you can find Covington, but be very careful with the map, son."

Lewis slowly unfolded it. Everything with print on it was important to Father and Mother. Like Bill, Lewis already knew the alphabet.

He looked intently at the map. The biggest words caught his eyes first. "P-U-T-A-W-A-T-O-M-I-E." He spelled the letters carefully.

"Oh, that is the Putawotomie Indian Reservation," Mr. Wallace explained.

"Indians? Are we going there?" Lewis asked.

"No, they still hold those lands, and will stay— unless the squatters force us to send them west," his father explained. "Look farther down the page for Covington."

"K-A-N-K-A," Lewis started to spell. The letters seemed to jump up and down with the jogging carriage.

"Kankakee, Lewis, another Indian word. The Kankakee Pond and River are the Indians' fishing grounds."

Lewis liked the sound. He thought he would like to fish there, too. "Kankakee, Kankakee, Kankakee," he repeated, in rhythm with the horses' hoofbeats.

Suddenly shouts and bellows interrupted his sing-song chant. As the carriage rounded a curve, a great cloud of dust came toward them.

"It's a herd of cattle being driven to market in Cincinnati," his father yelled.

Instantly he steered the carriage to one side. The wheels hit a stump, and the carriage shook wildly. Lewis almost bounced from his seat. He looked around excitedly at the passing herd. Cattle drovers were calling and singing out to the noisy, bellowing mass.

Lewis glanced back to watch the end of the procession. The carriage started with a jerk, as his father steered it into the road again.

Just then the boy noticed a package topple from the rest of the luggage, and slide toward the rear. He jumped up, landing on top and reaching for the bundle, just as it started over the side.

"Father! Stop the carriage!" Lewis shouted.

His father reined in the horses sharply, and the sudden stop sent both boy and bundle tumbling into the dusty road.

His father reined in the horses sharply, and the sudden stop sent both boy and bundle tumbling into the dusty road.

"My books!" his father exclaimed with surprise, as he jumped from the carriage and saw the bundle's contents scattered about. "You saved my books, Lewis. Are you hurt?"

"I'm alright," he replied.

"What is the matter, David?" Mrs. Wallace called from the carriage door. Then she saw her dusty boy. "Goodness, Lewis, let me clean your face! You had better come inside. Bill can ride on top awhile."

Lewis did not care much about being clean. Travelers always looked dusty, and he climbed inside reluctantly. It seemed warmer there than sitting under the sun.

John and Baby Edwin were asleep. Lewis rested his head on the high, black woolen seat. It was hot and dusty. Soon he was nodding with the motion of the carriage, and his head felt very hot and heavy.

He wished Grandmother Wallace were here to tell him a story. She always began the same way. He could almost hear her. Soon sleeping, and dreaming, he heard her in his dreams:

"When I was your age, Lewis, George Washington rocked me on his knee and told me about his adventures. He was a wonderful man, just like my Uncle John.

"Your great, great-uncle John Paul Jones, was strong and brave. He hated slavery, and he quit his job as chief mate on a slave ship."

Lewis thought he would hate slavery too.

"John Paul Jones raised the first American flag at sea, and whipped the enemy." Grandmother always ended with the Admiral's famous words: "Sir, I have not yet begun to fight."

Lewis liked to repeat them. "Grandmother, I have not yet begun to fight, but I will—I will—I will—"

The rest of his journey was filled with feverish dreams. Wagon wheels and hoofbeats pounded and thumped in his head. He was deathly sick for days with the dreaded illness scarlet fever.

"Lewis, Lewis." His mother's voice seemed far away. Dimly he saw her bending over him. Had she been crying? Her eyes brimmed with tears.

"Here, drink this," she said, giving him a cup of saffron tea. He felt her hand on his forehead. "The fever is broken at last! Oh, Lewis, you fought it so bravely!"

"We are here, in Covington," Bill said as he came over to the bedside. "But John is not," he added, swallowing hard.

Lewis looked at his mother. "What did Bill mean, John is not?"

"Oh," she said hesitantly. "You and John had scarlet fever on the trip. John did not get well. God is taking care of him now." She smiled at her son. "I am so glad He left you with us."

Chapter 3

Voice of the River

On the first Sunday in their new home, Lewis explored the attic. He was certainly glad to be out of the boarding house where they had stayed since coming to Covington. This small frame cottage was not as fine as their house in Brookville. Covington was a town on the frontier, where many buildings were built of logs.

Earlier that day the family had gone to the little church, where his mother was the only woman who knelt during prayer. Everything seemed different from Brookville.

"Only the sky and the trees are the same," he thought, while looking out of the small attic window. Now he could see a silver streak through the treetops. He wondered if it was the river and decided to go find out.

Quickly he climbed over trunks and boxes and scurried down the steep attic stairs. His mother was writing at the table in the front room. Her foot was gently rocking Baby Edwin, asleep in the low cradle beside her. Lewis missed John.

Lewis glanced out the open doorway. The sun made a bright carpet on the plank floor and shone on the book shelves along the opposite wall. A Wabash bedstead stood in one corner. His father's desk and easy chair were in another.

He came over to the table and watched the quill pen move along the large sheet of paper. "What are you writing, Mother?"

"A letter to your Grandmother Test at Lawrenceburg. I must tell her about our new home."

"Read the letter to me." Lewis wished he could read and write letters. He and Bill would be starting school soon, his mother had said.

She began reading. "This is the first Sunday I have been in a house of my own—not large, but very comfortable. There are porches, a smokehouse, and all such conveniences."

She glanced up. "Your Grandmother will be glad to know we are finally settled. I must tell her that your father is doing well, too."

Mr. Wallace was a silent partner in his brother Frank's store, here in Covington. The salary of a lawyer and lieutenant governor was scarcely enough for a growing family.

Mrs. Wallace continued. "People are very kind here, but every day of my life I am more convinced of the folly of setting our hearts on the things of the world."

"What do you mean by that?" Lewis asked.

"Oh, perhaps we think too much about things like houses and fine clothes. Today in church the ladies kept their white dresses neat, instead of kneeling to thank God for this beautiful country."

Lewis remembered that he would like to see this beautiful country. "I'm going for a walk," he called, skipping out the door.

He ran in his bare feet through meadows and wheat fields. Towheaded Lewis' hair was the same color as the ripening grain. He scarcely showed above the grass.

He felt at home here, under the warm sun so close to the earth and its thick carpet. He soon found the Wabash River. The current called softly.

His steps slowed among the twisted roots of grapevines and sycamore trees along the bank. The sun filtered down through overhanging willow branches, heavy with their full green growth.

A whippoorwill called. Cautiously he looked around and across the broad, deep stream. A long, flat bulk of logs and poles was coming slowly toward him. Something was moving on it.

"Who's there?" a voice called. "Who's there?" it called again. The river was coming closer now, lapping against the boy's ankles as the barge drew nearer and nearer.

The man on the barge looked a bit like his grandfather. He bent over the long oar, then tied the boat to a low willow limb.

"Well, well, Little Towhead, are you expecting a ride on my ferry?" the man called.

Lewis ran over to the barge. "Where are you going?" he asked.

"Just back and forth, ferrying folks across the Wabash. Some people traveling the National Road cross here. I can't say it's much of a road yet. What's your name, son?" the man asked.

"Lewis. I'm named for my Uncle Sam."

"Well, Mr. Lewis, that's a good name, but who's your Uncle Sam?"

"Major Samuel Lewis, of the United States Army. I'm going to be in the army, too."

"What's your name, Mister?" Lewis asked.

"Nebeker. Call me Nebeker, the ferryman."

Lewis liked Nebeker and his boat from the beginning. He had found a friend in Covington.

Early every morning after breakfast, Lewis went down to the Wabash River, rain or shine. It called to him in all of its moods—when it flowed gently on a

Nebeker and Lewis plied the ferry together and
explored the banks of the Wabash River.

bright day, or when it was a wild turbulent flood after
a heavy storm. Nebeker and Lewis plied the ferry
together and explored the banks of the Wabash River.

"Here are prints of a 'coon,'" Nebeker explained,
pointing to the flat footprints along the river bank.
"Looking for a crawfish, or a frog, to take the
young'uns. How they yip and yell at night, wanting to
know about everything."

The adventurous boy watched for the wary animals who slept during the daytime.

"There are the marks of a 'possum," Lewis said excitedly. "I can see the five toes plainly here in the mud. What does it eat?"

"It grows fat on fish and frogs, and the mulberries and persimmons overhead."

Lewis caught minnows to bait Nebeker's lines and splashed among grapevines at the water's edge. He climbed them, and swung out over the river, to dive into its cool depths. He floated with the current and swam against it. Soon he loved the Wabash and all of its creatures.

He would swing the oar with Nebeker, or lean over the low gunwale and watch the water move silently along. "Where does it come from? Where is it going?" he asked.

"God put it all here, Lewis. 'The Earth is the Lord's, and the fullness thereof.'" Nebeker sounded like his mother, when she read from the Bible.

"You learn to love the trees, and the earth, and the river, when you know He made them. You can feel mighty close to Him here," Nebeker said.

The boy thought so, too. The voice of the river had taught him many things.

Chapter 4

The Magic Pencil

"Quiet, children, quiet!" The schoolmaster's shouting rose above the clamor of young voices. "Quiet, I say!" The teacher rapped on his pine table with a hickory stick. The first day at school for the Wallace boys had begun.

Mrs. Wallace had brought Lewis and Bill to the little red brick building on a hill southeast of town. The boys were armed with Webster Spellers, slates, and bluestone pencils.

Lewis was delighted with the slate and chalk. Soon he was busy drawing a picture of the little girl seated on the bench beside him.

"Order, order!" The teacher called loudly. "See this rod?" He held the stick high. "No licking—no learning's my motto!" The stick came down on the table with a thunderous bang. It snapped in the middle, and one end flew over the heads of the children. The big boys roared. The little ones giggled.

"There are plenty more where this came from," the teacher said with a frown. His red hair seemed to stand on end as he went to the corner for another rod.

Lewis saw a bundle of rods there. Hurriedly he tucked the slate beneath him and sat on it. The pencil he laid on the bench beside the little girl. Now the teacher was striding down the aisle.

"Show me your books and pencils. Everybody needs a pencil in my school." He stopped at Lewis's bench. "Where's your pencil?"

Lewis reached for the chalk. It was not there. He stooped and looked under the bench. No pencil was in sight. As he sat up, he noticed the little girl beside him was chewing fast. A blue smudge was on her lips. Could she have eaten the chalk?

He didn't know what to say. "I—I must have lost it." He was telling the truth. The chalk really was lost so far as he was concerned.

Down came the switch on the boy's back. "I'll teach you not to lose your pencil!" the irate schoolmaster shouted.

Lewis felt the sharp sting. He wanted to cry, but held his breath instead. All the children were staring at him. He glanced at the little girl. She smiled sweetly, and the remains of the blue chalk showed on her teeth. She looked funny.

"Here, take my pencil," she whispered. "I brought two."

It was a pencil with real lead, much better for drawing pictures. This was worth the whipping he received.

At recess the children crowded around. They admired Lewis since he had taken his first beating without a whimper.

"Draw my picture, draw mine," they begged, and Lewis easily sketched his classmate's faces. Carefully, skillfully, he made light, short strokes, or broad heavy ones. Soon there was a picture on the paper, which looked just like the subject he was drawing. Some day he would draw pictures with words with equal skill.

"How do you do it?" the children asked.

"I don't know, but it's fun. It's easy. I love to draw pictures."

"It must be a magic pencil," the youngsters whispered.

The pencil did work magically in his fingers. Many pictures crowded his thoughts. The river and all of its beauty called to him. Sometimes his feet led him there instead of inside the schoolroom.

"You'll get a whipping!" Bill said, when Lewis would turn and bolt at the schoolhouse door.

"Nebeker and the river teach me more than old Redhead!" Lewis called back to Bill. Soon Lewis and

At recess the children crowded around.

his magic pencil would be drawing by the river.

One day, when Lewis was on the ferry, Nebeker was called to carry a load from the other side. Travelers signaled for the ferry with a horn, when it was on the townward side of the river.

Now someone was blowing the horn impatiently.

"Man your oar," Nebeker called to Lewis. "That traveler's in a hurry to cross."

Instantly the boy took his station at the oar, and glanced toward the opposite bank. A stranger on horseback led a team of oxen pulling a heavy wagon. A group of cattle followed the wagon.

"What's the fare?" the traveler called.

"A two-horse wagon, four bits. A man on horseback, one shilling. Cattle, each head, four cents," Nebeker answered.

"Hogs and sheep, two cents each," Lewis added wisely.

"I'd pay ten times the price, in good Mexican dollars, to get away from that varmint Black Hawk!" the stranger shouted.

"Black Hawk!" Lewis and Nebeker cried.

"Illinois's in an uproar. Black Hawk and a thousand Sauk warriors are killing every settler they can get hold of. This squatter has had enough of frontier living." The traveler wiped his brow. "The quicker you can get me across this river, the better."

"We'll take the wagon first," Nebeker called to the young boy driving the oxen. Slowly the clumsy beasts backed the wagon onto the ferry. A woman holding a baby sat beside the boy.

"Have you seen Black Hawk?" Lewis eagerly asked the boy.

"No, but we've heard plenty of tales about him. We're heading back home. He won't get us there. Captain Lincoln's been drilling the militia, but we're taking no chances."

"Well, my father's a soldier. He drilled militia in Brookville. He'll protect us," Lewis proudly replied. He wished he could see Black Hawk, though, and draw his picture—draw it with the magic pencil.

Chapter 5

Be Prepared

The alarm sounded in Indiana a few weeks later. Only thirty miles away two settlers had been killed by Black Hawk's fighters. The Bloody Three-Hundred mounted militia left the state capitol for Chicago. School was cancelled on the day some volunteers gathered in Covington.

Lewis watched excitedly as the companies formed and galloped away. Some men had squirrel rifles, and others wore muskets on their backs. A powder horn or a shot pouch hung from each saddle.

The boy longed to see the soldiers fight, to draw pictures of battle. One morning before breakfast he was busy with pencil and paper, sitting on his father's big easy chair. "They just look like sticks of wood," he said, half aloud. "I want them to fight!"

His father entered the front room. "Lewis, you should be learning your lessons. You are wasting your time with pictures."

Lewis glanced up. Colonel Wallace was wearing his West Point uniform, a gray frock coat with shiny bullet buttons.

"Father! Are you going after Black Hawk?" Lewis asked.

"I'm organizing a company of militia. A man must be prepared to fight for his country." Colonel Wallace inspected his gun, and strapped it into place.

"Father, I want a gun," begged Lewis.

"I'll teach you how to use one first. Go and see if my horse is ready."

Ball was at the gate, being groomed by a boy from the livery barn.

"He's here," Lewis called, "all ready." He started to pat Ball's nose. Lewis loved horses. "I'll have one some day, just like Ball," he remarked to the boy, "with a fancy saddle, too."

Colonel Wallace came out and inspected his horse. "You've curried him well. Have you checked his shoes?" the Colonel asked.

"This one is loose. Walk him over to the black-smith. Hurry, we drill in an hour." Colonel Wallace lost no time in giving orders.

"Yes, sir," the boy replied, as he led Ball away.

"Lewis, you can polish my boots here on the porch, after breakfast," Colonel Wallace added.

"Yes, sir!" His father commanded respect, especially when he was in uniform. Lewis followed him to the kitchen, where Bill was helping his mother at the hearth.

"Come, sit down, breakfast is ready," she said.

"Bow your heads, boys, while your mother says grace."

"Father, did you say grace at West Point?" Lewis asked, when the prayer ended.

"We sang grace there. The hall rang with the sound," Colonel Wallace recalled with pleasure.

"But I thought you learned to fight," Bill remarked teasingly.

"We learned the whole duty of man. There are other ways of defending your country and your honor. The law is one."

"Your father graduated with honor," Mrs. Wallace remarked proudly. "He ranked high in all of his studies."

"I will always be grateful to William Henry Harrison for my appointment to West Point."

"Tell us about it again," Lewis asked.

"Well, your Grandfather Wallace and General Harrison were friends and neighbors when they lived in Cincinnati. Your grandfather furnished supplies for Harrison's troops during the War of 1812. When Harrison went to Congress, he gave me the appointment to West Point that he had intended for his own son."

Colonel Wallace rose from the table and kissed his wife. "A good breakfast, my dear."

"Will you be away very long?" Mrs. Wallace smiled up at him.

"We are just drilling today, down in the lowlands. See if Ball is outside, Lewis, and don't forget to polish my boots."

As he went to the porch, Lewis remembered what his father had said. The soldiers would drill in the lowlands. He could watch them from the hill above without being seen. Then he would know how to draw soldiers in action!

"Hey, sonny, is your father inside?" A group of men was coming toward the house.

"He'll be out soon," Lewis replied.

Now the town square was filling with people from all over the county. The scare of an Indian attack had brought many to seek shelter within its friendly borders.

"Folks say they're building a blockhouse near Elkhart," Lewis overheard one man say.

"We might need one too. Black Hawk's trying to rouse the Miamis up north," another said.

"Can't blame Black Hawk for his uprising—those ornery squatters burned out his village and stole his corn. No wonder he's on the warpath."

Lewis continued to listen.

"He broke his treaty, though. Can't trust him. As

long as the lands belonged to the Government, the Indians could live and hunt there. Now settlers are buying land. The Indians got paid for it, a thousand dollars a year."

"Yeah, law's law, and the settlers had a right to protection."

Soldiers were everywhere now. Lewis thought they looked strange. Some wore hunters' jackets, some homespun shirts, and others had on faded uniforms.

Their hats would frighten anybody: straw hats with chicken feathers; wide brims with rooster plumes on top; and they carried swords, muskets, even hickory sticks and corn stalks!

"Fall in! Count off!" Colonel Wallace commanded from his place at the head of the column. "Right face! Forward march!"

The Colonel wheeled his horse to one side. Others on horseback followed. The bass drum gave a thunderous roll. Smaller drums echoed it. Two fifes struck up a marching tune, and the company started briskly down the street. Townspeople waved and shouted and dogs barked.

High above fluttered the stripes of red and white. A field of navy blue showed twenty-three stars as the American flag led them on. Lewis was thrilled to see it waving there. General Washington had carried it first, and John Paul Jones had raised it at sea.

Soldiers were everywhere now . . .

The young boy was sure that it would lead him, too. The flag was almost out of sight when Lewis took a shortcut to the hill.

Soon Lewis was crouching in the tall weeds above the lowlands. The Company came into view. It halted and wheeled into position.

"Present arms!" Colonel Wallace commanded.

Lewis watched the inspection. The soldiers directly below faced the hillside where he hid. He watched them cock and aim their guns.

They were aiming directly at the hillside, right at the spot where he hid! There was no time to run or even call out. What should he do? What had his father said? "A soldier must be prepared."

Lewis threw himself flat on the ground, just as the Colonel called, "Fire!"

At once, bullets whizzed by, dangerously close to his ears. Just as quickly he was on his feet, running with all his strength, before the company had time to reload and aim.

"Must have been a rabbit we scared away," Lewis heard one of the men exclaim, as he darted through the tall grass.

Lewis chuckled. The man thought he was a rabbit. He could run like a rabbit, and he did. Up the hill and through the town he went, straight home. Now he could draw pictures of soldiers in action.

Chapter 6

Scottish Chiefs

Young Lewis soon discovered that, like the soldiers, he must be prepared in many ways. Before his first school year ended, he was reading everything he could find.

One day he noticed a large sign nailed to the siding of Uncle Frank's store. The large letters spelled CIRCUS.

"A circus? What's a circus?" Lewis asked his uncle in the doorway.

"Well, in this one, animals and people perform, while a band plays. Best entertainment there is. Everybody in the county will be here next week," Uncle Frank explained to the eager boy.

"Come on, Bill," Lewis said to his brother on Circus Day, "let's walk down the road to meet it. I can hear the band already."

Soon the parade came in view. The band wore red uniforms trimmed in sparkling tinsel. Horns blew and drums beat, until Lewis thought the instruments would burst.

"There's a real bear in that cage!" Lewis shouted excitedly, as the boys skipped happily along and watched the circus folks prepare for the show.

Uncle Frank was right. It was the grandest show Lewis had ever seen. "Wouldn't it be fun to be like circus people?" Lewis asked his brother. "Circus people must have exciting adventures as they travel around the country."

In school, his adventures were just beginning. During the next school term, his first geography book showed him the world. Stranger than the lands in the book was the new teacher—a woman! The big boys were insulted at the idea. How could a woman dare teach?

Lewis thought differently when he looked toward the corner where the rods were kept. The switches were gone!

The backless benches were as hard as ever. The windows still had no panes. The fireplace offered as little warmth as ever. School was just the same, but the hickory sticks were gone. Lewis wondered how a woman teacher would keep order.

"Here is a book you may enjoy, Lewis," the teacher said, smiling, as she placed Olney's Modern Geography in his hands. "And here is a sum book."

"There's a real bear in that cage," Lewis shouted
excitedly. . . .

Lewis opened the geography first. It had pictures.
There was George Washington and an Indian. Other
strangers stared at him. He read below the pictures.

". . . the Scriptures inform us that they are the off-
spring of one common parent; that the delicate European

and the swarthy Ethiopian are brothers. . ."

He turned the pages eagerly. The world was so large, and round! Here was a drawing which proved it and a large word, A-S-T-R-O-N-O-M-Y. He liked the sound of large words. Then he found a small one, A-S-I-A, and read on:

"It was in Asia that our first parents were created,

and there occurred the most noted transactions." He wondered what that big word meant and continued:

He turned some pages and read again:

"Turkey comprises some of the finest and fairest regions of Asia. Within its limits have transpired some of the most as-ton-ish-ing events recorded in history." What big words!

"Children, come to your books. We will have arithmetic now," the teacher called, just as Lewis started to explore Turkey.

He opened the sum book. It had no pictures. Drawing numbers was boring. He drew pictures on the side.

The teacher noticed. "Lew Wallace, how can you ever make any money if you do not learn your sums?" she scolded. "There is a time for doing everything. 'To everything there is a season, and a time to every purpose under heaven.' You must learn that. 'Take care of the minutes and the hours will take care of themselves.'"

She came over to his bench. "Here, Lewis, put this on." She handed him a woman's sunbonnet, a horror of starched ruffles!

"Sit on the other side, with the girls, and say to yourself ten times: 'Take care of the minutes, and the hours will take care of themselves.'"

Lewis donned the sunbonnet. The class giggled.

He got hotter and hotter under the stiff headgear. It was a disgrace to be dressed like a girl! This was a hard lesson.

"Take care of the minutes, and the hours will take care of themselves." What did it mean? His father had said to be prepared. Did this mean learning that horrid arithmetic?

He wished he were in Turkey, or with the boy in Peter Parley's stories who had run away and gone to sea. Sometimes he pretended he had gone to sea when he was down at the Wabash.

The next day, Lewis ran there after breakfast, when his mother was busy at the hearth. He returned late for dinner in the evening. He was tired and dirty, but his eyes sparkled, and his face glowed.

"Where have you been, Lewis?" Mrs. Wallace asked anxiously. "I was worried about you."

"Shipwrecked, and picked up by Christians, just like the boy in Peter Parley's story," Lewis replied joyfully.

"What can I do with such a boy?" his mother wondered. One day she had an idea. "Here is a book which will keep you busy for awhile." She selected one of her husband's treasures.

It was a big book, the biggest Lewis had ever seen next to the family Bible. It was *Scottish Chiefs*, by Jane Porter. "Could women write books, too?" he thought. He climbed into his father's big easy chair and opened the book.

Lewis read slowly. "Bright was the summer of 1296. The war, which had desolated Scotland, was then at end—" He read on. In the third paragraph the name of William Wallace caught his eye. Why that was brother Bill! "We're Scottish chiefs, too," Lewis thought.

"But, Bill," Lewis excitedly said to his brother that night, after they had gone to bed. "You must read this book!"

"What's it about?"

"Scottish chiefs, our relatives. One of them has your name. The book tells how they fought to free Scotland. We can have battles just like theirs! We'll need more soldiers, though."

"Well, there's Wes Harper and Bob Evans and maybe Henderson Rawles," Bill suggested.

Next morning after breakfast, the boy prepared to fight for the glory of Scotland.

"We can make helmets of pasteboard."

"We need swords, too," Lewis replied, picking up some kindling by the smokehouse. "I'll take these down to the hide-out. Tell the boys to meet us there."

"Horses, what can we use for horses?" Lewis thought as he ran through the dense grass and flowering ironweed. "That will make a good horse, with a plumed tail." He pulled up some of the hard stalks.

Soon the boys were ready to fight.

"You can be Robert Bruce," Bill announced to Bob Evans.

"Bill will be Sir William Wallace," Lewis proposed. "I'll be Lord Bothwell. Wes can be Edwin, Sir William's friend."

"Who will I be?" asked Henderson Rawles.

"The brave Kirkpatrick!" Lewis said. "Everybody grab a sword. On to battle!"

They waved their swords and shields through the tall sunflowers. They struck down and trampled their enemies, the stalks of mullen, elder, and lobelias which grew along the way.

"With God's blessing, these wars shall be ended," cried Lewis, using the words of the book.

"We take the heart of Bruce to Palestine!" shouted Edwin.

"A soldier of the Cross betrays none who trust him!" Sir William exclaimed. "We have driven back the enemy. Retire, men, to the cliffs of Bothwell Castle!"

The boys sat on the hillside to rest.

"I wonder if the men in the story really were our relatives," Bill remarked.

"We can fight just like they do," Lewis answered.

Chapter 7

Winter Storm

Autumn touched the world with gold and wild fruit ripened. Bright leaves of towering beech, oak, and maple trees came down in showers.

With his mother's net shopping bag slung over his shoulder, Lewis went to gather the golden harvest. Lush, ripe pawpaws hung at arm's reach.

Lewis picked one, and bit into the soft, ripe fruit. "Um, as good as persimmons," he thought, "and twice the size." He ate his fill, and stored several in his bag.

Thick clusters of wild grapes hung from a pine tree. He climbed it to reach the fragrant bunches. His dog, waiting below, barked and wagged his tail.

"Here, Nuts, you might like grapes too," Lewis called, as he tossed him a bunch and shinnied down the tree.

"Come on, Nuts, we'll be back tomorrow for chestnuts and apples." Lewis picked up some of the bright leaves scattered about. "I can draw these—if only I

The dog trotted happily by his master.

had paints to color them."

The dog trotted happily by his master. They had been constant companions from the day they first met.

Lewis had been walking along the road one day earlier that summer when he had heard the whimpering cries of a puppy. The poor puppy had been run over by a wagon. Lewis patted him.

"Nuts, you'll be all right soon," Lewis said as he carefully picked up the limp puppy. One leg was broken. Lewis carried the puppy home and lovingly restored his health. A slight limp did not affect the puppy's speed as he raced along with his young master.

Big boys at school made fun of the limping animal. One day Lewis caught them throwing stones. "Stop hurting my dog!" he cried.

Lewis tackled the large boys. Fists flew, arms and legs swung as he tried to ward off the heavy blows. Lewis grabbed the bushy hair of one of the big boys hitting him. Both fell to the ground. Lewis held firmly to his attacker.

"Ouch! Stop pulling my hair," the boy yelled, as he jerked away, kicking Lewis as he ran.

Half-stunned, Lewis lay there. The puppy came over and licked his face.

"Well, Nuts, we lost our first fight," he sighed, "but here is something to remember it." He looked at a wad of bushy hair, still tightly clutched in his fist. "I'll tie this to your collar. It is my first battle trophy!"

With the coming of winter, snow and ice covered the hills. Lewis enjoyed sledding.

Otherwise Christmas had been dismal. The road from Indianapolis was impassable, and his father was stuck there.

Lewis was looking out of the window a week later, studying the lace patterns of frost on the handblown panes. Suddenly, he heard a blast from the town horn, announcing the arrival of the overdue stagecoach.

"Mother, the stage has come at last!"

"Run down to the store. Perhaps there is a letter from your father," Mrs. Wallace called.

The boy quickly donned cap and coat and hurried out. "Come on, Nuts," he called to his dog.

The coming of the stagecoach, which brought contact with the outside world, caused great excitement. Covington had no newspaper, and so people eagerly awaited travelers, the driver and the mail.

At the general store, the shopkeeper was opening the big leather mailbag in the doorway. People crowded around. Lewis listened. At last the Postmaster called, "Here's a letter for Mrs. Esther F. Wallace, postmarked Indianapolis, December 29th. Must be from your dad, Lewis."

Everybody was eager to hear from the lieutenant governor about the progress of the roads and canals. Covington expected to become one of the biggest ports in Indiana.

"Thanks, Mister." Lewis and the dog quickly ran home. His mother smiled as he handed her the letter. She had not smiled for so long, he thought. Chores of keeping house in the wilderness had worn away her energy and laughter.

She read eagerly as the boys crowded around the table in the front room.

Lewis ran down to the general store.

"Your father hopes to get home in four more weeks! 'We shall again be happy,' he says. He is going to bring me a pair of gaiters. He hopes they will keep my feet dry, but he doesn't know my size. Just like a man! He wishes us a Happy New Year. How I wish it could be!" Mrs. Wallace sighed as she folded the letter.

Lewis had been reading along with her. He enjoyed reading. Lewis was reading the books in his father's library. He copied the words and maps in the West Point books.

As a regular pupil at school now, he spent much time reading and drawing. There was nothing else exciting—nothing except the day when he learned about inventions.

That day some of the townsmen carted into the schoolroom a huge, black bowl, like a giant's pipe with a curving stem.

"Now the room will be warmer, children," the teacher explained. "This is an iron stove, a wonderful invention of Benjamin Franklin. The fire is here in the iron box. Smoke goes up the chimney through this pipe."

The word "invention" was new and interesting to Lewis. What else could be invented with iron?

Winter was a time for dreaming and thinking. Shut in by heavy snows, the boys would lie on the Persian rug beside the fireplace. Lewis liked the pattern of a lion woven in it. The rug had been brought from Brookville. Such a rug was a treasure here in the wilderness.

It was early candle lighting time. "Tell us a story," Lewis said to the hired girl. Their mother had fallen ill and could not tell stories or read to them.

The hired girl liked to tell the story of Covington's only murder and the hanging that followed.

"His ghost still walks. On moonlight nights it's sitting there on the platform where he was hung! Say the magic words or it'll haunt you!"

She would end her story with the words and wild

gestures. "Listen to that dog of yours now, howling there by the window. Sure now somebody's going to die!"

Lewis was impatient with her strange ideas. "Magic words! Magic is something wonderful like drawing pictures—not ghosts or frightening things!" he thought.

One night, Lewis fell asleep on the hearthrug while reading.

"Wake up, Lewis," Mrs. Hawkins, a neighbor was calling. "Your mother is dying." Lewis could not believe what he heard. Bill, already at the bedside, was crying bitterly. His mother's face was drawn and ashen.

"Mother, Mother," Lewis called. She did not answer. The light had left his mother's beautiful brown eyes. The awful meaning of the moment stayed with him. His father was away in New York. There was no one to care about his utter loneliness. The funeral, with its black pointed coffin and mournful songs, did not ease it.

He missed his mother's hand on his forehead, pushing back the stubborn locks. He missed her gaze of wonder, as she looked at him, perplexed by the spirited nature that sent him on so many adventures.

Their home was broken now. The boys boarded with the John Hawkins family. "Winter is cruel and hard," Lewis thought. "I wish spring would come soon."

Chapter 8

College-in-the-Woods

Two years passed and soon Lewis was nine. As he sat on the riverbank, he was as troubled as the swirling waters of the Wabash, swollen by spring rains.

Lewis missed Bill, now going to school at the new College-in-the-Woods of Crawfordsville. What kind of school was it? Did a boy learn to shoot and hunt and scout in the woods?

Questions rushed through his mind like the swift current along the bank. A turtledove called overhead. "Come away, away," it seemed to warble. Should he go? Should he leave the river he loved?

"Go away, river, good-by!" he said, as he tossed a stone into the muddy water and made up his mind. "I am going to see Bill, and go to College-in-the-Woods."

Uncle Milton was making a trip to Crawfordsville that very day. "If I meet him on the way, he'll have to take me along," Lewis decided.

For two miles he walked, trousers faded and torn,

shirt buttonless, feet bare.

He waited and finally Uncle Milton came along on horseback. "What are you doing here, Lewis?" he said with great surprise.

"Going to Crawfordsville with you. I'm going to see Bill and go to college," Lewis replied.

Uncle Milton burst out laughing. Lewis was used to having folks laugh at him, though they never laughed at Bill.

"I declare, Lewis, you are always thinking, or dreaming of something. That wonder-box of yours is never quiet a minute, but come along." Uncle Milton half-heartedly hauled Lewis up behind the saddle.

The twenty-eight miles of riding all day were tiresome, but Lewis dreamed of scouting and hunting with Bill at the college.

"Here we are," Uncle Milton announced, when he left his nephew at the door of Forest Hall.

Lewis looked up at the building, set among tall walnut and maple trees. Below the trees, clusters of dogwood and redbud lifted their flowering branches to the sun.

"Is this the College-in-the-Woods?" he wondered. People coming from the building did not look like hunters.

"Where are you going, sonny?" one of the people asked Lewis.

"Nowhere. I've just come." Lewis answered.

"What's your name?" the student continued.

"Lewis Wallace. I've come to see my brother, sir," Lewis answered politely.

"Hmm. Son of the lieutenant governor." Lewis noticed the man raise his eyebrows. Others were smiling. Lewis tugged at his trousers and wiped his face on his sleeve.

"Run and find the young man's brother," someone said.

Bill was as surprised as Uncle Milton had been at the sight of Lewis, but he did not laugh. "Why, Lew, when did you come?"

"Just now, with Uncle Milton," Lewis replied.

"What for? Come on, I'll take you to my boarding house for a good scrubbing," Bill chuckled.

"But I want to go to the college in the woods," Lewis insisted to Bill.

"All right. You may come to class after you are cleaned up." Bill promised.

Lessons in grammar, and arithmetic were the same for him as they were for high school boys.

"This is no place for me," Lewis decided. He soon discovered a stream called Sugar Creek and explored the bluffs and hills around it. "Almost like the Wabash," he thought.

One day at his boarding house he overheard something which made him curious.

"The Elstons have imported a new musical machine! They are having a grand party tonight. They have invited folks to hear it." Lew heard one man telling another.

"First, the horsehair sofa, and now—this musical contraption! Imagine carting such a thing here in a Conestoga wagon!" the second man commented.

"Must have cost a pretty penny, bringing it all the way from New Orleans, but money's no matter with Major Elston. He's the richest man in the county, maybe in the state. He owns a town, too, besides his mills and store. Lives in a real castle, like a gentleman."

The remark about a castle made Lewis start to wonder. "Could it be a castle like those in Scotland? What sort of an invention was a musical machine? I think I should go tonight to find out. He said people were invited."

The night and the moon were friendly when he started toward Elston Castle that evening. People were walking up the long lane.

Finally a large white house stood before him, lit up like a birthday cake. The grand party was in progress, and the curious boy stole quietly under a parlor window. He peered over the sill, eyes popping with wonder.

The chandelier sparkled with dozens of candles. People were moving about in frilly dresses and frock coats. He had never seen people decked out so gaily.

Soon a lovely young girl came over to a large, wooden box on legs. She sat down and opened the lid. Her fingers began to play the machine!

"Come over to the piano and sing," he heard her say. Then he saw another young girl. His heart jumped! A little princess with golden curls was singing now, a song that Lewis knew:

"One little, two little, three little Indians."

He had seen a princess—and a piano!

His curiosity was satisfied. "One little, two little, three little Indians," Lewis whistled all the way home. He had seen things to dream about that night, but he would not tell Bill his secret.

Not long after his exciting night in Crawfordsville, the Kerr family, with whom he was boarding, moved to the country.

Lewis moved with them. His father, disappointed in Lewis' schoolwork, thought he might learn to farm.

The chores—hoeing corn, milking cows, churning butter—made Lewis restless.

"Would you like to read?" Mr. Kerr suggested when he noticed the boy looking at the books on the parlor table. "My library's not big, but there's some good reading here."

"Come over to the piano and sing," he heard her say.

Lewis looked at the books—*Plutarch's Lives, The Bible,* and *Daniel Boone.* "I've heard stories about Daniel Boone hunting and living in the woods. I'll read this one first."

"How would you like to go squirrel hunting with me? Reckon I might go tomorrow."

"Squirrel hunting? Really, Mr. Kerr?" The boy's face beamed. "Will you teach me to shoot?"

"Sure enough," Mr. Kerr promised.

Lewis soon handled his rifle like an expert. He

supplied the family table with game daily.

"You've learned fast, Lewis," Mr. Kerr proudly remarked to his pupil. To his wife he said, "Quite a marksman, that boy, and a bookworm, too." He shook his head. "I never saw the like."

Lewis roamed the forest, a gun in one hand, a book in the other. He was a scout now, living like Daniel Boone. Building a fire with flint, he roasted ears of corn, munched wild cherries, and went to the spring for a drink.

Strong and tanned, the boy looked like the young Indians of the neighboring county. "This is truly my college-in-the-woods," he thought happily.

Several days after Christmas, Lewis found Bill waiting for him when he returned from a hunting trip. Bill seemed excited about something.

"Come and hurry, Lew, father is at the inn, and—"

"Why, Bill, what's the matter?"

"Father has brought us a—" Bill hesitated.

"A what?" Lewis grew impatient.

"Father has brought us a new—"

"A new what?" Lewis demanded.

"A new mother!" Bill blurted out finally.

The word struck like thunder from a clear sky. Sparks of lightning burst into flame. "Well, she may be your mother, but she's not mine! I won't go!" Lewis announced.

But Lewis did go, clean and quietly.

"This is your new mother," Mr. Wallace said of the pretty young lady beside him. "We will all be together now, here in Crawfordsville."

Over and over to himself Lewis kept saying, "She's not my mother, not my mother," while he plodded blindly along the trail in the woods. The day was bitterly cold. Wind stung like icy fingers through his thin clothing.

"Go away, wind," he said, turning homeward.

The icy blast left its fury within him. That night, and for many nights, his moaning and coughing brought the new mother quickly to his bedside. He felt her hand, soft and gentle, on his forehead. She bent over and kissed him.

"Thank you, Mother," he whispered. The word seemed natural now.

Chapter 9

The Magic Touch

"A proper name, an inspired name, Indianapolis!" So Jeremiah Sullivan had said when he thought of the name for the new state capital.

Planted in a swampy forest, the little log town was growing into a real city by 1837, as though a magic wand had touched each tall tree, turning it into a building.

Lewis's father had been elected governor, and the family moved to Indianapolis. Exploring it, the ten-year-old Lewis was as thrilled with the sights as Judge Sullivan had been with his name "Indianapolis."

People hurried everywhere. Wagons, carts, and carriages with parasoled ladies were bumping over the muddy streets.

Many folks went in and out of Washington Hall, the biggest hotel in town. Members of the legislature were gathered there to plan roads and canals.

Shouting, digging, and shoveling, brawny workmen were laboring to dig the roads and canals. Saws and hammers hummed and pounded to build houses and stores.

"How wide this street is! Big enough for a battle-field," Lewis thought. Red flannel banners blew like battle flags above the stores, to draw trade. Lewis gazed into the shop windows as he walked down the south side of Washington Street.

He stopped to look longingly at a saddle, decorated with silver trappings, which hung from a pole above a shop door. The sign on the doorway said, WILLIAM ECKERT—SADDLES, HARNESS & TRUNKS. Another sign said, C. AND J. COX, TINNERS—TIN CHURNS.

He hurried on to EVANS CONFECTIONARY, and read the list of wares on a chalkboard: CANDIES, CORDIALS, CAKES, FRUITS, CHEESE, NUTS, TOYS, & ICE CREAM. With his nose against the window, as if trying to smell the contents, he gazed at the tall jars of rock candy and peppermint sticks.

He was tempted to go inside but was due at the Post Office across the street to pick up the mail. Turning away, he glanced in the next shop win-dow: JAMISON, MILLER & COMPANY. BEAVER AND OTTER HATS, FINE SEAL CAPS, BLACK AND DRAB SILK HATS, FINE AND COMMON BROWN HATS, COMMON SEAL AND CLOTH

CAPS, BRUSH HATS, CHILDREN'S HATS.

"Hats, hats, hats! Does everybody wear a hat in the city?" he thought, disgustedly.

Soon he was wearing one himself.

"Boys wear hats to church, Lewis," Mrs. Wallace stated, when she outfitted the governor's sons with Sunday clothes, hats included.

"Remove your hats when you enter," the boys were told as they entered the church.

Boyish energy was harnessed upright in the hard benches. Lewis felt the starch in his stiff collar. His trousers were tight, too. He held tightly to the slippery black oilcloth hat. How he longed for the Wabash, where he felt closer to God than sitting here on the hard bench.

The hat was so shiny he could see himself in it. Like a mirror, it showed the faces around him. He had an idea.

From his vest pocket he took a pencil. Soon he was drawing faces on the top of the hat. "If only I had paints to color them," he thought.

Opportunity came the day Lewis learned the governor was having his portrait painted. Jacob Cox, the tinner who made churns, was painting it in his spare time.

"I've come to see my father's picture," Lewis announced to Mr. Cox.

"You must be one of the Wallace boys." The artist glanced up from his work. He was bent over, grinding colors on a marble slab.

"Is this the way you make paints?" the boy looked intently at the process. His fingers were itching now.

"It is out here in the West. Then you mix the powder with oil." Mr. Cox explained.

"I could help you with the grinding," Lewis suggested hopefully.

"So you could. The first thing an artist learns is how to mix colors and shades. Do you want to be an artist?" asked Mr. Cox.

"Well." Lewis stopped. Should he tell Mr. Cox how much he wanted to be an artist? Perhaps the man would laugh. "I will help you now," Lewis replied.

Carefully he watched and learned how to grind and mix the colors. "It's almost like magic, Mr. Cox, the way you make paints and put them into a picture."

Lewis watched as Mr. Cox painted, and soon his fingers were itching to paint. He picked up a tin pan, dabbed some colors on it, and slipped it under his coat. "See you tomorrow, Mr. Cox." He hurried out the door and home to the attic.

Their house was a large two-story frame, near the canal south of Washington Street. This was not the Governor's mansion. The first governor's wife had shunned the house on the Circle, which Lewis thought

He found a wooden box under the eaves to use for a canvas.

looked like a castle. There was no place to hang the family laundry or to stable the horses.

"What does that matter?" Lewis said to himself. "Our attic is a wonderful place for my very special secret."

He ran up the stairs without being seen, the tin pan clutched tightly under his coat. He found a wooden box under the eaves to use for a canvas. He placed his tin palette beside it.

"The colors will have to be thinned with oil. Where can I find some oil?" he asked himself.

The doctor had left some castor oil for the hired girl that very morning. "It should be in the kitchen cupboard, where the medicines are kept," he thought. Quickly he dashed downstairs. He found the right bottle.

"Lewis Wallace, what do you want?"

The greasy bottle almost slipped from his grasp as the hired girl took him by surprise.

"A—a—a cookie!" he stammered, thinking quickly. One hand reached toward the cookie jar. The other clutched the bottle, which he hastily tucked under his vest. Just as quickly he ran from the kitchen.

"Whew, Nuts," he whistled, "that was a close call, but we kept our secret, and we're almost ready to paint."

"I'll just need a brush. Where can I find a brush,

Nuts?" He looked at the wagging tail.

"Come here, chum, you have just what I need! I'll have a brush as soon as I can find a scissors, a stick, and a piece of string."

At last the young artist was doing what he enjoyed most, painting at every chance. Lewis watched Mr. Cox whenever the young boy ground the colors for the artist. Then Lewis hurried home to the attic.

A picture of an Indian, which he had admired in a book, was almost finished. A bright red turban framed the rugged face. Golden hoops hung from his ears. His right eye, blinded by a hunting accident, was closed. It seemed to be winking at the young artist. Tenskatawa, the Prophet of the Shawnees, who tried to save his race from destruction, alone shared the boy's secret. Their hideaway was safe, or almost.

Mrs. Wallace was a tidy woman. Inspecting the attic one day, she noted a very odd smell—castor oil!

"Lewis, did you take the castor oil?" She came into the sitting room, holding the picture for all the family to see.

The governor looked at the one-eyed portrait and burst into a laugh. "That Indian must have had a good dose of castor oil!" he said jokingly.

Lewis ran to the attic for escape, and the family followed. His secret was now discovered. At the sight of the makeshift studio, his father laughed again.

Then he became serious.

"Lewis, you must give it up! Artists starve! You cannot make a living by painting pictures."

"But—Mr. Cox—" Lewis began.

"Jacob Cox has a trade. He paints in his spare time. A great painter must have people who like art well enough to pay for it. The education of an artist costs money. You have neither." Mr. Wallace patiently explained to his ambitious son.

Lewis was silent. He knew Jacob Cox was a fine artist. Surely someday people would appreciate him. Perhaps he should have confided in Mr. Cox. Perhaps he should have asked for the castor oil instead of just taking it.

"Honesty is the best policy," the governor always said.

Chapter 10

The Treasure

The county seminary was famous for its stern teacher and the ball players who kept the schoolyard alive with a rough game called shinny.

"High buck or low doe," the captain called. The wooden ball was thrown high in the air or low on the ground. The struggle to knock it home with the hard maple shinny stick created bruises and black eyes.

The game of shinny continued until the school bell rang. Then the players deposited their sticks and balls in the hallway, and fidgeted in the schoolroom.

Lewis Wallace, now eleven, fidgeted with them, played ball with them, and had a rousing good time. But his fingers were still itching to draw, as they would one day itch to write. One afternoon at recess, he used the blackboard as his canvas.

He sketched the picture of a rabbit—a very real rabbit with the face of his teacher. Of course he intended to erase it, but the schoolmaster returned too soon.

He sketched a picture of a rabbit—a very real rabbit
with the face of his teacher.

The class roared. Surprised, the teacher looked
around. His eyes looked first at the picture and then
at Lewis. The beating that followed brought blood
running down the boy's legs and tears to his eyes.

"Wipe it off the board," he commanded, starting at
the boy with fury.

Lewis felt the blood tricking down his legs. He
was breathing heavily. An open window was behind
him. He jumped out and ran, straight to the house
of his friend, Farmer Taffe. Breathless, he burst into

the farmhouse kitchen.

"Why, Lew, you've taken a beating! What for this time?" Mr. Taffe asked.

"For drawing a picture, Mr. Taffe! This is the last time. Nobody likes my art. It just gets me into trouble," Lewis spoke sadly.

"That teacher has no taste for art, or a sense of humor, either," Mr. Taffe replied, as he took a jar of salve from the kitchen cupboard.

"Here, Lewis, let's doctor those legs now. Lie down on that old trunk in the corner."

The farmer bent over the boy to look at his swollen legs. "That confounded scoundrel! To beat you like this! Not fit for trainin' a horse."

"Have you ever trained horses, Mr. Taffe?"

"Well, I know enough about training a horse to realize that each one is a little different. First thing you do is get close to him, talk to him a little, and find out what he's meant to be, a work horse or a pacer."

"I'm going to have a horse some day, a pacer, or a trotter, or maybe a single stepper."

"Well, it takes a little time and patience to train a horse, or a boy. Most of all, it takes love. A young colt will soon learn to love the master that loves it."

"None of my teachers ever tried to find out what I'm meant to be. I'd like to be an artist, but I'm through, now." The blow to the boy's talent stung deeper than the cuts from the teacher's whip.

"Don't ever give up what you like to do best. Just wait until the right time comes," the farmer advised.

Lewis was wondering what he would become several days later on his way to school. He stopped at the fence which enclosed the State House lawn. He was disappointed and lonesome. School had blotted out his beautiful dream of becoming an artist.

He gazed at the State House, which seemed like a palace the first time he saw it. That was almost a year ago. The tan stucco still glistened like gold against the stately white pillars. He decided to go inside. Perhaps the governor could answer the questions running through his mind.

Up the curved stairway he climbed to the second floor. The governor's offices were on the east. Lewis glanced in. His father was talking with some men.

One man was saying, "The panic this county has been in for the past year is going to ruin us and the whole plan for the roads and canals." Another complained, "Everyone has lost faith. Money is worthless!"

The boy remembered how his father had talked when he took the oath of office. He had called upon the lawmakers to spend the state's money wisely, and especially for education.

"Education is closely connected with the prosperity and success of any people," Governor Wallace said repeatedly.

"Education?" Lewis thought. How could he get an education? What would he become? His father was too busy to talk about it. Now he seemed busier all the time and scarcely laughed any more.

The lonesome boy noticed an open door across from the governor's office. Light came through the tall windows.

He went in cautiously. No one was there. The carpet felt soft and inviting. He stood in the middle of the room and looked around, slowly, in amazement.

Books, books, and more books! Everywhere they lined the walls, reaching from the floor to the high ceiling above. The room was filled with books! To him, it was a treasure house!

He wanted to reach out and touch all of them at once. His fingers were itching, just as they did when he wanted to draw.

A stepladder was in one corner, to reach the highest shelves. The boy climbed it and sat on the top. Now each book took shape before him.

Carefully he took the first one from the top shelf. *The Railroad Journal.* There were four volumes, with pictures of inventions! He replaced it for another, and another.

Franklin's Works, Jefferson's Works, Webster's

The room was filled with books!

Speeches. He glanced at the next row of shelves. He saw *The Last of the Mohicans.* "An Indian story! I will read this one first." Then his eyes traveled down the shelves to a book with the picture of a knight in armor. Ivanhoe, he read on the cover.

He continued scanning the shelves: *Letters From Constantinople, Letters From Russia, Captain Ross's Second Voyage, Conquest of Florida.* "Goodness, will I ever conquer all of these books?" he wondered. Then he heard someone enter the room.

Lewis glanced down. He had forgotten about school, dinner, and seeing his father.

"Why, Master Wallace, you seem interested in our State Library."

Lewis recognized the man with the high forehead, smiling up at him. It was the secretary of state. "Have you read all of these books, Mr. Brown?" he asked.

"As state librarian, I have to know them, and care for them. I ordered the books from Cincinnati. I spent the money well and have a little left, too."

"Do all states have libraries like this?" Lewis asked Mr. Brown.

"Ours is one of the first, and best, if I do say so." Mr. Brown spoke with pride.

"I'm going to read all of these books, if you will let me," Lewis said proudly.

"You might become smarter than the governor, if

you do," Mr. Brown said with a wink. He was known for his funny sayings. "Would you like to borrow a good book? Your father and I are almost ready to leave."

The boy reached for *The Last of the Mohicans* and thought, "A librarian must be an important person to know about so many books. He is important enough to be the secretary of state!"

Chapter 11

Turning Point

Again and again twelve-year-old Lewis returned to the State Library. He examined every book for its pictures. Soon he had looked at several hundred.

"Well, Master Lewis, your name is on the borrower's list more times than any other. You're our best patron!" the Librarian remarked.

At every chance the determined boy stole away to read in the woods or the old deserted mill down in Fall Creek Bottom.

Daydreaming, he became the Black Knight, the Red Rover, or Natty Bumpo. He fought their battles, lived their adventures, and longed for the time when he would be as daring and brave as his heroes. At school he became the worst student in arithmetic.

"What can I do about his schooling?" Governor Wallace worriedly asked his wife.

"Lew is a bright boy, reading all the time," she promptly answered. "He is a dreamer, just different from Bill. Perhaps the teacher does not understand him."

"Our schools need teachers who take time to understand children and help them. I must do something to raise our standards of education. Next January I am calling all the teachers to a convention. What do you say to that, dear?" Governor Wallace asked.

"Splendid, and I hope you will give the women a voice in it. They deserve equal rights, and the vote. A young lady teacher in New York, Susan Anthony, is starting the movement." Mrs. Wallace replied.

"Women equal to men? Women voting? Nonsense, the legislators would say. Why, women have as much chance as—ten thousand mice!" David Wallace exclaimed.

"Never mind, dear. Some day we shall have the vote and see that our children are properly educated." Mrs. Wallace spoke sincerely.

"With your help, Mrs. Wallace, that may be so. For the present, I am responsible for educating our children. I have always spoken for education. In my last message, I praised the Wayne County Teachers. They have been the first to give dignity and importance to their profession!" he said in turn.

"Well, Governor, I hope you find the right teacher for your son," Mrs. Wallace replied.

"I have it—I know the very man, Professor Hoshour.

He is a trustee of the State College," explained Governor Wallace.

"State university now," she reminded him.

"That is right. We made Bloomington College a university last February. Well, I am making some progress. There are great leaders in this state—Wiley, Maxwell, Hoshour, and others. Yes, I will send Lewis to Centerville Seminary to learn from Mr. Hoshour."

"Centerville? Why, the boy could board with his Uncle Charles in his big house."

"A good idea. You seem to be filled with them. But women voting! Well, I have the deepest respect for them. The time may come."

A few days later, the boys traveled to Centerville, seventy miles east by the National Road. Adventure-loving Lewis, accompanied by Bill, was sent to board with Aunt Rebecca and her husband, Judge Charles H. Test.

Professor Samuel K. Hoshour taught students from the best families of the state. Among them were the son of an Indian Chief, a black boy, two orphans, the Morton brothers, the daughter of the town doctor, and a young man from Tennessee. The latter amused the students by his Southern drawl and funny poems.

Shortly after the term began, he jotted down some verses and passed them along to the next student. The next student in turn passed the poem along to be read.

The Professor looked over his spectacles, when he heard the giggles that followed. Then he watched, while the students, unaware, passed the paper along the aisle.

"Will someone kindly read the message aloud?" The professor was pulling at his cheek, a habit that meant he was disturbed.

At this point, right when the teacher was speaking, someone passed it on to Lewis. He stared at it uneasily.

"Read it aloud, Master Lewis, so we may all enjoy the contents," commanded the teacher.

Lewis swallowed and took a deep breath. He arose, shoulders erect. The class was wrapped in silence as he read loudly and clearly, with meaning in each word:

"'O Lord, preserve us every hour
From the rod of S.K. Hoshour.'"

All eyes were on the teacher. His stern features burst into a broad smile. "You speak very well, very well, Master Lewis. Did you write this?"

"No, sir. I just read it, as you directed," answered Lewis.

"It was well written, clear and to the point. Now let me guess who wrote the poem—could it be our young gentleman from Tennessee?"

The teacher gazed at the tall Southerner, who was half-slouched in his seat, trying to make his lanky legs and arms invisible.

"Uh, yes, suh, Professor, Ah penned it a while back, suh."

"Well, young man, continue writing your poetry! I shall continue using my rod, whenever it is needed.

"Master Wallace, I like the way you read. I would be obliged if you would come to my house this evening. My wife runs our bookstore. We have some books you might enjoy."

"Books? A bookstore? Shelves of books like those at the State Library?" Lewis' black eyes lit up with pleasure. "Yes, sir," he added, "I will certainly be there tonight. Thank you, sir."

"Tell me, young man, what do you enjoy doing?" the professor asked his caller that evening. It was his way of getting acquainted with his many students.

"Oh, I like to read, hike in the woods, and go hunting and fishing," answered Lewis.

"Fine! I used to hunt, too—opossums in the hills of Pennsylvania. What kinds of books do you enjoy?" the professor questioned Lewis.

"I like adventure stories, and books about people, like Plutarch's *Lives*. I read all of Scott's and Cooper's and Washington Irving's books in the State Library. I know every book on the shelves there," Lewis added proudly.

"Why, Lewis, you have read more books than most grownups!" He was delighted to meet such a well-read pupil.

The professor went to the shelf for a book. "If you enjoy Washington Irving, you should read the books of Oliver Goldsmith. They are excellent English! Here, take this one with you."

Lewis looked at the title. *The Vicar of Wakefield* was printed on the cover.

"Washington Irving read that book and later wrote like Goldsmith. Have you ever thought of writing?" suggested Mr. Hoshour.

"No one ever told me I had talent for anything," Lewis answered slowly.

"Oh, everyone has some skill. You just have to discover what it is. You read well. You speak well. You can write well, too," insisted the professor.

Lewis sat quietly, listening. This teacher had told him he could do something well.

"Now here are the rules for good writing," the teacher continued. He handed another book to his student. "These are the *Lectures of John Quincy Adams*. Were you to ask me which of the rules is most important, I would say the whole secret of writing is this: *Everything must be clearly stated, everything.* Remember that, Lewis. You can become a good writer some day."

The boy, overwhelmed, picked up the books and went toward the door. "Become a writer?" he thought. "That is certainly something to consider."

"Here is another book—our finest use of the English language, the most amazing adventure story in the world." Professor Hoshour handed Lewis a *New Testament.* "There, read that, the story of the birth of Jesus Christ!"

Lewis was ushered out of the room as though he were the governor. At the door, the teacher held a lamp over his head, to light his way.

"You must come again soon, my boy. We will work on arithmetic the next time. But dig away at those books, and study. A scholar is self-made, you know. Good-night." Professor Hoshour brought to a close an important evening.

Lewis went out into the night, strangely satisfied with this new and kindly teacher, who told him he could write. He would write—at least he would try.

The next morning Lewis had his head deep in a book as soon as he rose.

"Come on, Lew, hurry," Bill urged. "We'll be late for class."

Lewis, walking slowly to school, was trying to read

along the way. "Go ahead. I'll catch up with you." He sat down under a beech tree behind the schoolhouse and continued to read.

Facing Professor Hoshour after being absent was a difficult task for Lewis the following day.

"Lewis, the next time you are a truant, I will use my rod on you, in front of the class," the Professor firmly stated the next day. "Your father has sent you to me and paid me to give you an education. I must see that you get it!"

Reading under the budding beech trees called more strongly than the teacher's threat. Some time later, he spent a second day in the woods.

"Lew, you are sure to get a thrashing tomorrow!" Bill remarked.

"Well, it's worth it. I'll be prepared." Lewis felt confident.

The next morning he tied a broad shingle to his back, under his vest and coat. "That will give me a little protection," he thought.

"Master Lewis, you know my rule. Are you prepared for a whipping?" the Professor asked sternly.

"Does he know how well prepared I am?" Lewis thought. He took off his coat and marched to the teacher's desk, his back stiff as the board under his vest. He bent over, ready for the rod. As it came down heavily on the board, the rod snapped in the middle.

"Get me another rod, Lewis!"

The boy looked up. He had scarcely felt anything under the armor he wore. "Yes, sir," Lewis answered, and he noticed a slight twinkle in the teacher's eyes. Did the professor know the shingle was under his vest?

Again the rod came down. The physical pain was slight, but the boy's pride was hurt. "I will not return to any teacher who thrashes me!" he promised himself. Besides, he had learned what he wanted to do.

He was ready to return home, to study and write. Professor Hoshour had shown him the way to develop his talents.

Chapter 12

Pocahontas and Politics

Thursday, November 28, 1839, was the first Thanksgiving Day for the state of Indiana. David Wallace, governor, had proclaimed it.

In his proclamation, he asked that citizens attend their usual places of worship, to give thanks for their good harvest and health.

After church, the Wallace family gathered around the large dining table. At last they were living in the new Governor's Mansion.

The finest house in Indianapolis had been bought by the State from Dr. John Sanders, father of Mrs. Wallace. They could entertain three hundred guests in the large house.

"Bow your heads, boys. Your father will give the blessing," Mrs. Wallace commanded.

Twelve-year-old Lewis could hardly take his eyes from the tempting sight on the table, but he bowed his head. He thought his father, always long-winded, would never finish.

". . . And, in the words of my Thanksgiving Proclamation," the Governor continued, "We ask Thy protection and favor and Thy guidance in the ways of wisdom. We ask Thee to extend liberty to all nations, and the knowledge and influence of the Gospel. Amen."

"This is a good idea of yours, Father, to have a Thanksgiving Holiday," Lewis remarked over a big drumstick.

"You're just glad we have no school today," Bill retorted.

"We went to church instead. Besides, I am going to spend the day writing," Lewis replied.

"Grand," their father exclaimed. "I am grateful that *both* of you are doing well at the seminary now. I am proud of you Lewis, to see your poetry in the newspaper."

After the year under Professor Hoshour, the young author was a respected student and member of the English Club.

"We have much for which to be thankful," the Governor remarked. "The year ahead shows promise. We'll elect Harrison to be President."

"You are working harder for Harrison's election than your own," Mrs. Wallace said. "You are being blamed for these hard times. I hope people will learn the facts."

Twelve-year-old Lewis could hardly take his eyes from
the tempting sight on the table. . . .

"Never mind, dear. They will, sooner or later. By
next Thanksgiving, we will know how they feel," the
Governor added.

"Is this Thanksgiving just like the Pilgrims had,
with the Indians and Pocahontas?" eight-year-old
Edwin asked.

"Pocahontas was at Jamestown, Ed. The Pilgrims
had the first Thanksgiving at Plymouth!" Lewis
quickly stated.

"That reminds me," the Governor remarked. "The

play *Pocahontas*, by our friend Robert Dale Owen, is to be given again this winter. The author is directing Lindsay's Company from Cincinnati. Shall we go?"

"You know some church people do not approve," Mrs. Wallace replied.

"But this is a fine play, based on history. Why, the New York papers compared it to Shakespeare, when it played there last year. Easterners were surprised that it was written by 'a citizen of the West,' from Indiana."

"Browning's Hotel will be a better place to give it than Mr. Olleman's wagon shop, where the plays were held last year," Mrs. Wallace replied.

"Plays with real actors? Oh, Father, may we go?" Lewis begged.

Many people Lewis knew were helping with this grand event. Jacob Cox was painting the scenery. Jacob Dunn's mother was making costumes. William Brown's son Joe, now librarian, and James Jordan were acting. They met in the State Library to consult books and make plans.

"What fun it would be to act," Lewis thought, as he watched.

People came by the National Road and Central Canal to attend. The admission price of twenty-five cents was high, but articles of trade were accepted in place of cash.

The actors performed above footlight candles in tin cases. The orchestra, two fiddlers, played popular tunes: "Hang On," "Jay Bird," and "Fishers' Hornpipe." Young Lewis loved the fiddlers' music.

"Let's give our own plays next year," someone suggested. Then the city's first actors' club, The Thespian Corps, was formed. Lewis and Bill both became members.

"We can rent the scenery from William Lindsay," someone suggested.

"We will give *Pocahontas*, and Shakespeare, too," the young actors decided.

It was a year of fun and acting! The boys found many ways to study their parts.

"Come on, Bill, let's practice shooting our arrows over at the Hay Press. I have to kill a panther in the play, you know," Lewis proposed.

The Hay Press, where straw and hay were baled for shipment, was just west of the old frame building where the plays were given.

The boys practiced their lines along the way. Bill had the part of Pocahontas, and Lewis was her sister Numony.

"Imagine what we'll look like, dressed as a couple of Indian maids, with a feather in our wigs!" Lewis said laughingly. "We'll be a funny-looking pair. Yippee!" Lewis yelled. Then, clowning, he rehearsed his lines in a high-pitched voice, "Ah, Pocahontas, it is so natural a thing to love! So difficult to keep one's heart from loving!"

"Never mind, I'll act serious when the time comes. Plays are great! I think I'll write one and a poem about Pocahontas," added Lewis.

That summer the adults were acting seriously, too. The Whigs were united to elect William Henry Harrison President, and beat the "Locofocos." The slogan, "Tippecanoe and Tyler Too" rang through the woods that he had won years before. Party feeling was at a peak.

Young Lewis was agog as he watched the long wagon train head out toward the Michigan Road, bound for the great rally at Tippecanoe.

"Come on, Joe, let's join the parade." Lewis called excitedly.

"Do you think we should? What'll your Dad say?" replied his pal, Joseph Pope.

"Father's away. I can act in his place and help get Harrison elected. Come on, let's go!"

Lewis was barefooted, and his trousers were rolled to his knees. An old straw hat was on his head. He strutted along as if he were dressed in a West Point uniform. The boys led the way.

"Lew, you will have me laughing on the stage, if you don't act serious!" laughed Bill.

They glanced back to watch the endless wagon train. It crawled, snake-like, twenty-five miles long on the rough road. There were log cabins on wheels. There were dugout canoes. There were wagons piled high with barrels of cider, for the "log cabin and hard cider candidate."

People were on horseback. People were on foot. People were in carriages and covered wagons, twenty thousand or more. Lewis was sure there never had been such a celebration.

Folks were singing songs, sometimes making them up as they went along. The election of 1840 was the first where music and songs were used to rally the people.

Some one would start, then everybody joined in the singing:

"What has caused this great commotion,
Motion, motion, the country through?
It is the ball a' rolling on,
For Tippecanoe and Tyler too!
Van, Van is a used up man!"

"Hurrah for Harrison!" the crowd shouted.

"Look, Lew, that banner over there," Joe exclaimed. The boys, several yards ahead of the parade, were coming in to the first town, ten miles out. "What does that flag mean?"

"Democrats! Locofocos! They are making fun of

"Come on Joe, let's join the parade," Lewis called excitedly.

us!" Lewis shouted. He sprang like a squirrel up on the roof of the blacksmith shop where the pole was fastened. He tore it from its moorings, and then straddling it, rode the pole down to the ground.

Joyfully clutching his prize, he ran toward the head of the wagon train.

"What have we here?" Mr. Cole, the first driver asked, stopping his team.

The boys held up the long pole with a red petticoat dangling from the top. They described the glorious deed.

"Why, you're our heroes! Who are you, and where are you going?" Mr. Cole asked.

"To the convention, if you'll take us," Lewis replied joyfully.

"Get right in. I'll take you there and bring you back." Mr. Cole promised.

Lewis climbed to the high wagon seat, but Joe shook his head. "I—I'd better not go, Lew. I'll see you, when you get back."

"Well, good-by, Joe. You'll miss a big time, camping out for a week or more. Isn't that right, Mr. Cole?" Lewis was sure he should go to act in his father's place.

"Yes, sir-ee! We'll beat those Locofocos! Wait and see!" shouted Mr. Cole.

Day and night, Lewis did not miss a minute of the grand convention—the barbeques, the singing, the speaking, and the torchlight parades.

Outfitted by Mr. Cole in a new suit of clothes, he acted just as the Governor would, he thought.

The boy dreamed that someday he would be making speeches at conventions.

Weeks later, the newspapers related the happy results. William Henry Harrison was elected President! The Governor rejoiced. Then David Wallace prepared his own farewell address. The people had rejected him for re-election.

"You were just ahead of your time with your ideas," Mrs. Wallace said.

The family moved to a farmhouse out on the avenue. Lewis tended the garden and led the cows to pasture. David Wallace resumed his law practice. Now he had time to spend the long winter evenings at home with his family.

They sat before the big open hearth, with logs piled high beside it, while the father read them stories—stories of lords and ladies, of brave knights and battles.

The fourteen-year-old boy sat dreaming of a tale he was going to write. It would be about lords and ladies, knights and battles. He would call it *The Man-At-Arms: A Tale of the Tenth Century*. His first book.

Chapter 13

The Call to Arms

"FOR MEXICO. FALL IN" The large sign below the American flag fluttered from a window on Washington Street. Two fifes and a drum blew and beat to attract passers-by.

A tall youth, dark and handsome, was standing outside. "Come along and fight for Texas! Join the colors! Defend the United States," he called.

On May 12, 1846, Congress had declared war on Mexico. For months, for years, since Texas became independent, there had been unrest along the border. Disputes, foreign agents, and restless settlers forced an answer. That answer was war!

Nineteen-year-old Lew Wallace had followed the events from their beginning. Jim Bowie and Davy Crockett were his heroes, and they were in the thick of the action. The land south of the border had called to him since he was sixteen. He had read a new book in his father's library, *The Conquest of Mexico* by

William Prescott, that had completely captured him. From that time on, he had longed to see the fabled land. Now he was recruiting others to join him.

He had tried to see Mexico once before, when he was still sixteen. "Let's go and join Commodore Moore, of the Texan navy!" he proposed to a friend, Aquilla Cook.

"I'll do it," was the reply.

They got a skiff and loaded it with supplies, a rifle, and a shotgun.

They set off for New Orleans and Mexico, bound for adventure, until a constable and Dr. Sanders overtook them a few miles downstream.

Then David Wallace decided the time had come to take a firm hand with his adventure-loving son.

"Lewis, I want you to look at these papers," Mr. Wallace firmly stated, calling his son into the library. "Tell me what they are."

"Receipts for my school bills," the disappointed youth replied.

"Yes. I have tried to give you and your brothers what, in my opinion, is better than money—an education." He paused, and then continued, "Were I to die tonight, what I can leave you would not keep you a month! You *must*, from this very day, earn your own living! I am sorry and disappointed, but I still have hopes for you."

"Thank you, Father, for all you have done for me. I will not forget it. I hope I will not disappoint you," answered Lewis honestly.

Lew felt free, yet determined to make something of himself. What could he do? How could he earn any money? He turned to a friend of the family, Robert Duncan, the county clerk. Lew related his father's judgment.

"So you want to settle down, and get a job?" the county clerk asked.

"Yes, if I can," Lew agreed.

"You can. Come along," said the clerk.

The county clerk took him to the vault where records were stored. "We need complete copies of all of these. I'll give you ten cents for every hundred words you copy."

Soon Lew was earning good wages, eighteen dollars a week, and more with night work. He had learned to make fast, neat, and accurate copies. He celebrated his first pay by purchasing a rifle and going on a squirrel hunt. Life seemed carefree and pleasant.

Always popular with his friends, Lew enjoyed socials and musical evenings. He took a course in manners and dancing.

The carefree, pleasant life soon became tiresome. Lew found himself restless, uneasy, and longing for something more.

Late at night, locked in the vault of the clerk's office, he
wrote and studied by lamplight.

He remembered the words of Professor Hoshour,
that a scholar is self-made. He decided to study and

learn everything he could about Mexico. Then he could write another book. The first one was already finished and laid aside.

Late at night, locked in the vault of the clerk's office, he wrote and studied by lamplight. The land of Montezuma and Cortez took shape upon the pages. His book *The Fair God* was coming to life. He was fired with more energy than ever before.

Writing a book would take years, though, with no income in sight. What could he do? He could not spend his life copying words in the clerk's office. Lew considered becoming a lawyer.

Bill was studying law under his father, who had returned from Congress after failing to be reelected. Again David Wallace had been ahead of his times. He had cast the deciding vote in favor of Samuel Morse's invention of the telegraph. Folks laughed at the invention and criticized such a waste of money.

The law was a respected profession, although it had little appeal for young Lew. It demanded much study and practice, and it would be good training.

At night Lew labored over the heavy law books in his father's office. On Saturdays, his father drilled and examined him. Soon he was earning money by practicing before the Justice of the Peace. He had a part-time job as a newspaper reporter, and earned fees by helping legislators write bills and speeches.

The day approached for his final examination to become a lawyer.

Then the Mexican War began and all else was forgotten. He would defend the flag!

When Lew heard the news that the country was calling for volunteers, he rushed to the State House. "Will any troops be from Indiana?" he asked the adjutant general.

"Yes, that's what bothers me. We must furnish three regiments. The business is entirely new to me," answered the adjutant general.

"Can anyone raise a company?" Lewis was bursting now with eagerness.

"I suppose so. Then it can be mustered-in, and assigned by the governor."

"I'll do it, with your permission," Lew Wallace announced excitedly.

The would-be soldier had already trained with the Marion Rifles, a local militia company. He had studied Scott's *Infantry Tactics*. He decided he would rouse the boys of the disbanded militia, and join them together for real battle.

Now he was calling, "For Mexico. Fall in!" He had rented the room on Washington Street as a recruiting office. He had hired the fifers and drummer. For three days he recruited, until the company was formed. Officers were chosen. Lew Wallace became a second lieutenant.

His father was at his side now.

The company was soon ready to depart. Crowds gathered to bid them farewell. Speeches were made. The ladies presented a flag to the soldiers. Lew was thrilled, as he walked along in the parade. His father was at his side now. They silently walked along, tall and erect.

There were last minute handshakes. There were tears, and the ladies waved handkerchiefs. The moment of departure had come.

The father shook hands with his son. His smile showed his pride and approval. "Good-by," he said. "Come back a man."

The son had dreamed of glory under the stars and stripes, of gold in the mountains of Mexico, of the braid of an officer's uniform. He would come home with honor or not at all.

The End

What Happened Next?

- Lew Wallace returned from the Mexican War and became a lawyer and Indiana state senator.

- Between 1861 and 1865, he served in the Union Army during the Civil War and earned the rank of major general. He saved Cincinnati from falling into Confederate hands and played a key role in defending the city of Washington DC in 1864.

- In 1878, he became the governor of the territory of New Mexico.

- Lew's most famous novel, *Ben-Hur*, was published in 1880. More than 20 million people saw *Ben-Hur*, the play, which was performed continuously on Broadway from 1899–1921.

- In 1881, Lew Wallace traveled to Turkey as the American ambassador.

- Lew Wallace died in 1905.

For more information and further reading about Lew Wallace, visit the **Young Patriots Series** website at www.patriapress.com

More than 20 million people saw *Ben-Hur*, the play.

Fun Facts About Lew Wallace

- Lew Wallace was an inventor. He held a patent for a new kind of railroad tie and fishing pole.

- The naval hero John Paul Jones was Lew Wallace's great-great uncle.

- *Ben-Hur* was the best-selling novel of the 19th century and has never been out of print. It was filmed three times. The 1959 movie starring Charlton Heston won 11 Academy Awards.

When Lew Wallace Lived

Date	Event
1827	Lew is born in Brookville, Indiana • The first Mardi Gras is celebrated in New Orleans. • The Baltimore & Ohio Railroad becomes the first railroad in America to offer commercial transportation of both people and freight.
1836	Lew moves to Crawfordsville, Indiana to be with his brother. • Davy Crockett arrives in Texas and is killed in the Battle of the Alamo. • Charles Darwin collects scientific data on his ship, the HMS Beagle, which he will later use to develop his theory of evolution.
1846–1848	Lew serves in the Mexican War as the first lieutenant in the 1st Indiana infantry regiment. • The US declares war on Mexico with James K. Polk as president. • The Treaty of Guadalupe Hidalgo formally ends the war nearly two years after it began.

- The California gold rush begins in 1848.

1861   Lew is promoted to Major General in the Civil War.
- Abraham Lincoln becomes the 16th President of the United States.
- The Civil War begins in North Carolina at Fort Sumter.

1862–1865   Lew commands at the Battle of Shiloh
- Abraham Lincoln is assassinated in 1865
- The Civil War ends and slavery is abolished by the 13th amendment.

1873   Lew publishes his first book, *The Fair God*
- Jesse James and his gang committed the first successful train robbery in the American West.
- Budapest becomes the capitol of Hungary.

1878–1881   Lew serves as governor of the Territory of New Mexico
- *Ben Hur: A Tale of the Christ* is published in 1880 during Lew's term as governor.

- The American Red Cross is established

1881–1885   Lew is the U.S. Minister to the Ottoman Empire (Turkey)
- The Statue of Liberty arrives in New York City.
- Louis Pasteur tests his rabies vaccine.

1905   Lew dies in Crawfordsville, Indiana.
- Albert Einstein develops his theory of relativity.
- The Russian Revolution begins in St. Petersburg in 1905.

What Does That Mean?

Folly (p. 19)—an unwise or foolish idea

Gunwale (p. 22)—the edges on the sides of a boat

Fife (p. 33)—a high-pitched flute

Flint (p. 58)—a striking stone used as a tool to create fire

Churn (p. 61)—a container used to make cream or butter

Oilcloth (p. 62)—cotton fabric made waterproof with oil

Makeshift (p. 66)—a temporary substitute

Truant (p. 83)—a student who skips school

Proclamation (p. 85)—an official announcement

Agog (p. 90)—an excited state

Mooring (p. 92)—wire, ropes, or cables used to secure a vessel

Skiff (p. 97)—a small boat made for one person

About the Author

Author, poet, composer, musician and historical scholar, Martha E. Schaaf was a career librarian and teacher who set up more than 25 libraries throughout the country in the course of 15 moves with her husband, who was in the military. She received a BA degree from Indiana University, where she was responsible for helping open the previously all-male Student Union building to girls, and a master's degree from Columbia University. Born in Madison, Indiana, Martha is also the author of *Duke Ellington, Music Master.*

Books in the Young Patriots Series

Watch for more **Young Patriots** Coming Soon
Visit www.patriapress.com for updates!

LaVergne, TN USA
17 October 2010
201136LV00002B/2/P